A is for Activism
COLORING BOOK

School for Every Child

March

Xenial

Equality

Dream

Zeal

Kindness

Guerline Ladouceur Laurore

Dedication

This coloring book is dedicated to children and adults of all ages who dream to make this world a better place.

A is for Activism

A is for Activism: Helping everyone get the chance to do something important like go to school.

Read and trace the sentence

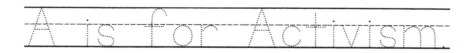

Draw your own picture of A is for Activism and use it in a sentence or write a short story about Activism.

B is for Bake Sale

B is for Bake Sale: Selling yummy treats to raise money for a good cause like to give books to children who need them.

Read and trace the sentence

Draw your own picture of B is for Bake Sale and use it in a sentence or write a short story about Bake Sale.

C is for Club

C is for Club: A club is a group of friends who work together to help others and make the world a better place. They come up with ideas and do activities to bring about good changes.

Read and trace the sentence

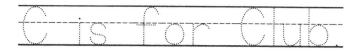

Draw your own picture of C is for Club and use it in a sentence or write a short story about Club.

D is for Dream

D is for Dream: Imagining a world where every child can go to school and learn.

Read and trace the sentence

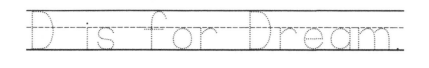

Draw your own picture of D is for Dream and use it in a sentence or write a short story about Dream.

E is for Equality

E is for Equality: Everyone gets to learn and play, no matter who they are.

Read and trace the sentence

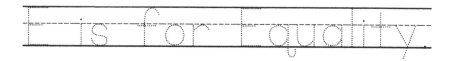

Draw your own picture of E is for Equality and use it
in a sentence or write a short story about Equality.

F is for Fundraiser

F is for Fundraiser: Gathering money through fun activities to help every kid go to school.

Read and trace the sentence

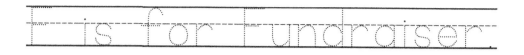

Draw your own picture of F is for Fundraiser and use it in a sentence or write a short story about Fundraiser.

G is for Giving

G is for Giving: Sharing what we have to help others go to school and learn.

Read and trace the sentence

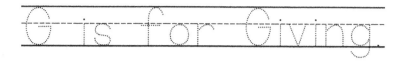

Draw your own picture of G is for Giving and use it in a sentence or write a short story about Giving.

H is for Helping

H is for Helping: Doing something to make things better for others, like making sure every child can go to school.

Read and trace the sentence

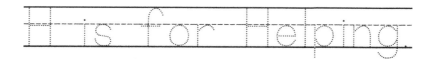

Draw your own picture of H is for Helping and use it in a sentence or write a short story about Helping.

I is for Inclusion

I is for Inclusion: Creating a space where every child feels welcome to play and learn together.

Read and trace the sentence

Draw your own picture of I is for Inclusion and use it in a sentence or write a short story about Inclusion.

J is for Journey

J is for Journey: The adventure of learning new things every day.

Read and trace the sentence

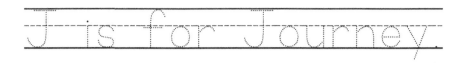

Draw your own picture of J is for Journey and use it in a sentence or write a short story about Journey.

K is for Kindness

K is for Kindness: Being nice and caring to everyone.

Read and trace the sentence

Draw your own picture of K is for kindness and use it in a sentence or write a short story about Kindness.

L is for Leader

L is for Leader: Being someone who helps friends work together for a good cause.

Read and trace the sentence

L is for Leader.

Draw your own picture of L is for Leader and use it in a sentence or write a short story about Leader.

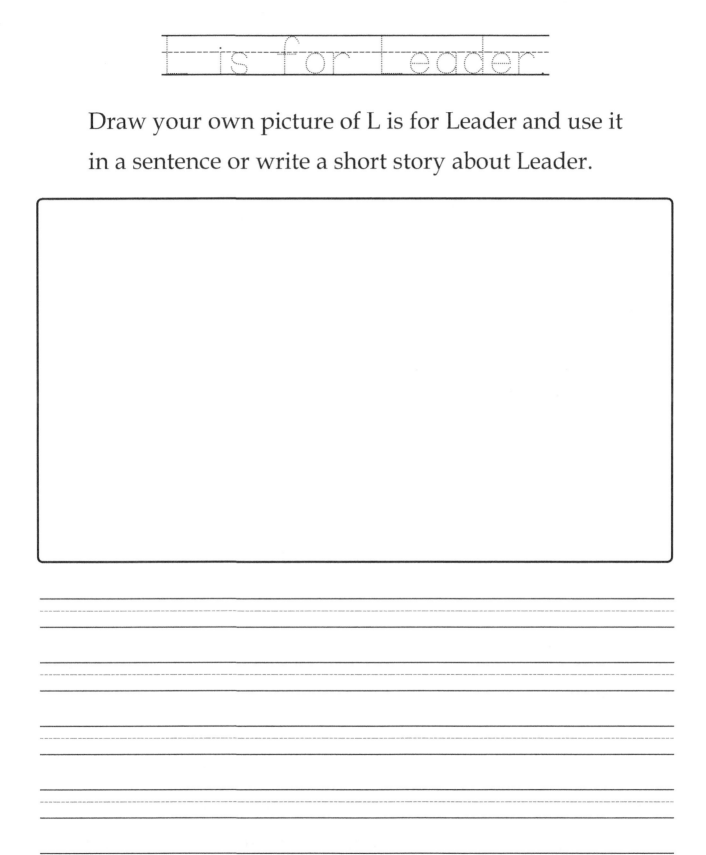

M is for March

M is for March: Walking together with friends to show we care about something important, like making sure every kid can go to school.

Read and trace the sentence

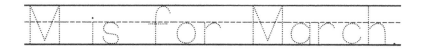

Draw your own picture of M is for March and use it in a sentence or write a short story about March.

N is for Nice

N is for Nice: Being extra kind and helping friends at school.

Read and trace the sentence

Draw your own picture of N is for Nice and use it
in a sentence or write a short story about Nice.

O is for Organize

O is for Organize: In activism, it means getting people together to do something good for everyone.

Read and trace the sentence

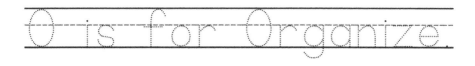

Draw your own picture of O is for Organize and use it in a sentence or write a short story about Organize.

P is for Protest

P is for Protest: Making signs and standing together to show we care about everyone learning.

Read and trace the sentence

Draw your own picture of P is for Protest and use it in a sentence or write a short story about Protest.

Q is for Questions

Q is for Questions: You ask about something because you want to learn more or understand better. It helps you learn and grow.

Read and trace the sentence

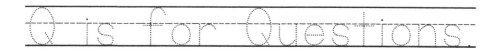

Draw your own picture of Q is for Questions and use it in a sentence or write a short story about Questions.

R is for Rally

R is for Rally: A rally is like a big party where we all cheer for something good, like helping everyone learn and have fun at school.

Read and trace the sentence

Draw your own picture of R is for Rally and use it in a sentence or write a short story about Rally.

S is for School

S is for School: A place where we go to learn and meet friends.

Read and trace the sentence

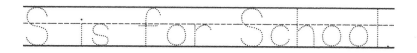

Draw your own picture of S is for School and use it
in a sentence or write a short story about School.

T is for Teamwork

T is for Teamwork: Joining with friends to make big changes, like helping everyone get to school.

Read and trace the sentence

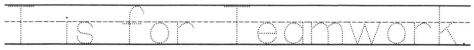

Draw your own picture of T is for Teamwork and use it in a sentence or write a short story about Teamwork.

U is for Unite

U is for Unite: Coming together for a big goal, like making sure every kid can learn at school.

Read and trace the sentence

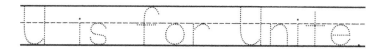

Draw your own picture of U is for Unite and use it
in a sentence or write a short story about Unite.

V is for Volunteer

V is for Volunteer: Helping others without expecting anything back.

Read and trace the sentence

V is for Volunteer.

Draw your own picture of V is for Volunteer and use it in a sentence or write a short story about Volunteer .

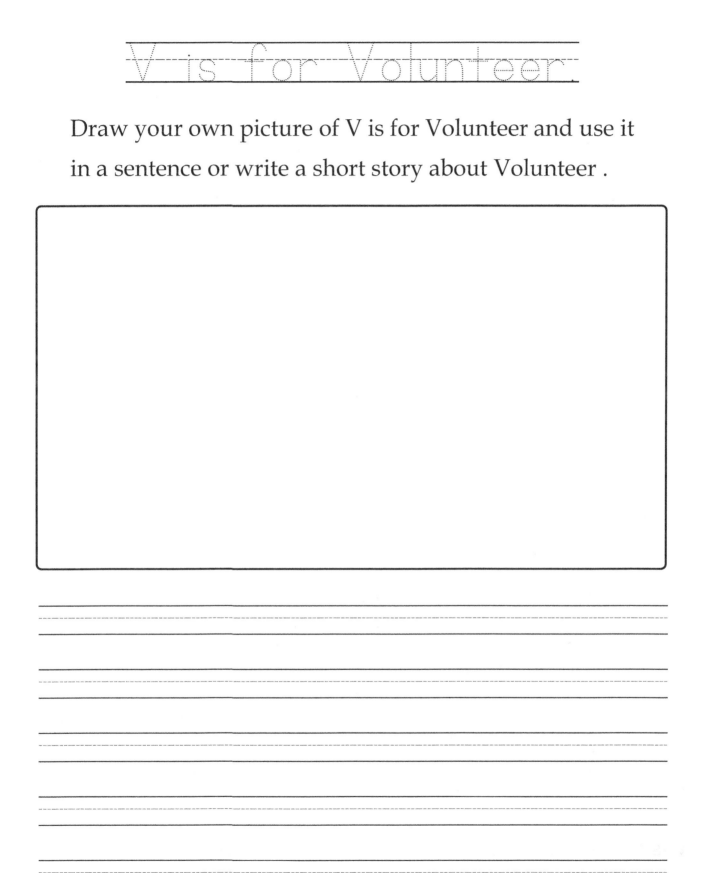

W is for World

W is for World: Our big home that we all share and try to care for.

Read and trace the sentence

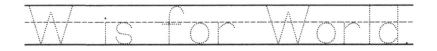

Draw your own picture of W is for World and use it in a sentence or write a short story about World.

X is for Xenial

X is for Xenial: Being welcoming, especially to people who are from another countries, by showing acceptance and kindness.

Read and trace the sentence

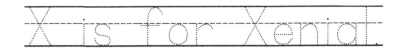

Draw your own picture of X is for Xenial and use it in a sentence or write a short story about Xenial.

Y is for Youth

Y is for Youth: Kids and teenagers who are full of energy and fresh ideas, ready to make the world a better place.

49

Read and trace the sentence

Y is for Youth.

Draw your own picture of Y is for Youth and use it
in a sentence or write a short story about Youth.

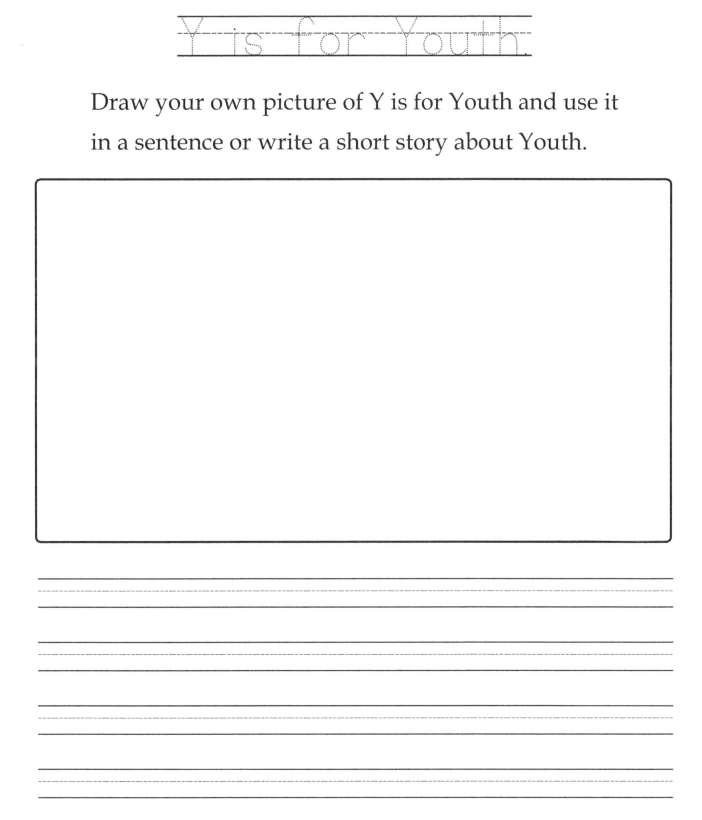

Z is for Zeal

Z is for Zeal: Being very excited about working on something very important.

Read and trace the sentence

Z is for Zeal.

Draw your own picture of Z is for Zeal and use it in a sentence or write a short story about Zeal.

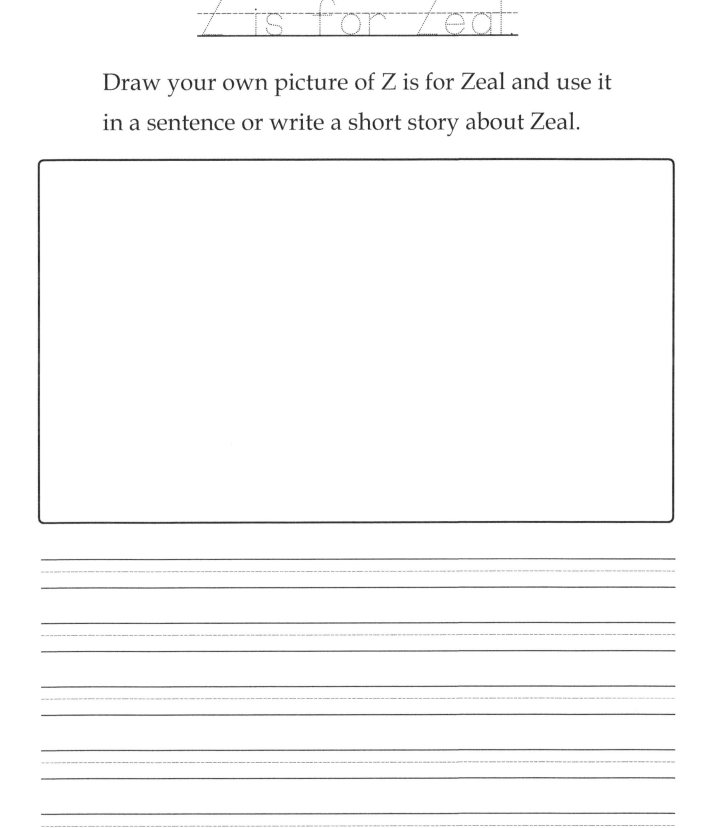

CERTIFICATE OF ACHIEVEMENT

THIS CERTIFICATE IS PRESENTED TO:

_____

For completing coloring book "A is for Activism" and learning vocabulary related to activism and understanding that every child has the power to make a difference in the world. Great job!

_____

Date

GUERLINE LADOUCEUR LAURORE, AUTHOR

PARENT/ TEACHER

GLL BOOKS ETC

About the Author
Guerline Ladouceur Laurore, MA, JD, MPA

Guerline is a fervent advocate for human rights and literacy, inspired by her Haitian roots and the educational challenges she observed there. Her commitment to education began by teaching her mother to read and nurturing a love for reading in her children, who showed exceptional literacy skills at an early age. Her book skillfully combines emergent reading techniques with the vital principle of education as a human right.

Her educational journey includes degrees in psychology and psychopathology from France, a Juris Doctorate from Widener University School of Law, and a master's in public administration from the University of Pennsylvania. Guerline is a Certified Human Rights and Human Trafficking Trainer and leads ISAFER, a human rights organization.

Guerline is multilingual, speaking English, Haitian Creole, French, Spanish, and Portuguese. Her career spans roles as an Educational Consultant, Attorney, Mediator, and DEI expert. She's active in her community, serving on the World Affairs Council of Harrisburg and as a member of Delta Sigma Theta Sorority, Inc., co-chairing their International Awareness and Involvement Committee. She's involved with the Greater Pocono Chapter of Jack and Jill of America Inc. Guerline lives in Central PA with her family, where they attend the Greater Zion Missionary Baptist Church.

59984975R00038